To Jordan
— Love, Mommy

For Edie Weinberg
— B.L.

Go to www.scholastic.com for Web site information
on Scholastic authors and illustrators.

Text copyright © 1999 by Grace Maccarone.
Illustrations copyright © 1999 by Betsy Lewin.
All rights reserved. Published by Scholastic Inc.
Printed in the U.S.A.

ISBN 0-439-45159-0

SCHOLASTIC, HELLO READER!, CARTWHEEL BOOKS, FIRST-GRADE FRIENDS,
and associated logos and designs are trademarks and/or registered
trademarks of Scholastic Inc.

1 2 3 4 5 6 7 8 9 10   24   11 10 09 08 07 06 05 04 03 02

The Class Trip

by Grace Maccarone
Illustrated by Betsy Lewin

SCHOLASTIC INC. Cartwheel ·B·O·O·K·S· ®

New York   Toronto   London   Auckland   Sydney
Mexico City   New Delhi   Hong Kong   Buenos Aires

The teacher says,
"It's time to go."
So she puts on her hat
with the polka-dot bow.

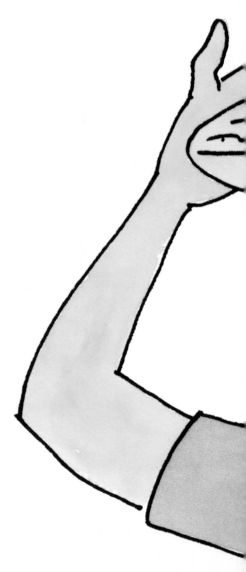

Then Sam, Jan, Pam,
Max, Kim, and Dan

get on the bus
as fast as they can.

They sit in seats
two by two.
They talk. They sing.

They're at the zoo.

Sam sees the chimps.
They fight. They play.

Sam's friends move on.
Sam wants to stay.

The teacher says,
"Sam, don't be slow.
Keep up with the group.
It's time to go."

Monkeys chatter.
They swing. They climb.

Sam is having
a wonderful time.

The teacher says,
"Sam, don't be slow.
Keep up with the group.
It's time to go."

Elephants walk.

Lions run.

Polar bears
enjoy the sun.
Sam is having
so much fun.

The teacher says,
"Sam, don't be slow.
Keep up with the group.
It's time to go."

Fish swim.

Frogs lea

Flowers float.

Turtles sleep.

Sam looks up
and has a scare.
Sam is alone.
His group is not there!

Which way did they go?
Sam does not know.
He looks up high.
He looks down low.
Sam tries to stand
on tippy-toe.

And that's when he sees
the polka-dot bow.
Sam runs to his teacher.

Now he will know
to stay with his group
and go, go, go, GO!